THIS BOOK BELONGS TO

GREYFRIARS BOBBY

A PUPPY'S TALE

STORY BY
MICHELLE SLOAN

ILLUSTRATIONS BY
ELENA BIA

One bright Edinburgh morning, a wee Skye terrier lifted his nose to the air and sniffed. He knew that smell!

A meaty waft of sizzling sausages drifted down to the Grassmarket.

The pup leaped up, shaking fleas onto his grubby straw bed.

He flew up the steps, past the night watchman, Constable John Gray, who was on his way home from work.

"Good morning wee Bobby," he said.

Bobby barked a cheery hello and carried on up to the top.

He squeezed through the railings of George Heriot's school and bolted across the yard, weaving his way through the playground games.
"Hello there wee Bobby," shouted the schoolboys.

All day long Bobby chased rats, and the old cook rewarded him with a fine, fat sausage.

When evening came, he trotted wearily back down the steps, past Constable John Gray, who was setting out for work.

"Goodnight wee Bobby," he said.

Bobby snuffled an exhausted goodnight and plodded back to his grubby straw bed.

But one dreich day, a new cook came to Heriot's school.
A fist-shaking, broom-shoving, cat-loving cook, who said,
"Get out of my kitchen, scruffy pup!"

Bobby trotted gloomily into Greyfriars kirkyard next door.

"Hello," said a boy. "I'm Sandy. Here, you can share these crumbs with the sparrows."

Bobby licked the crumbs gratefully from the boy's cold hands.

And when Sandy turned to go, Bobby followed.

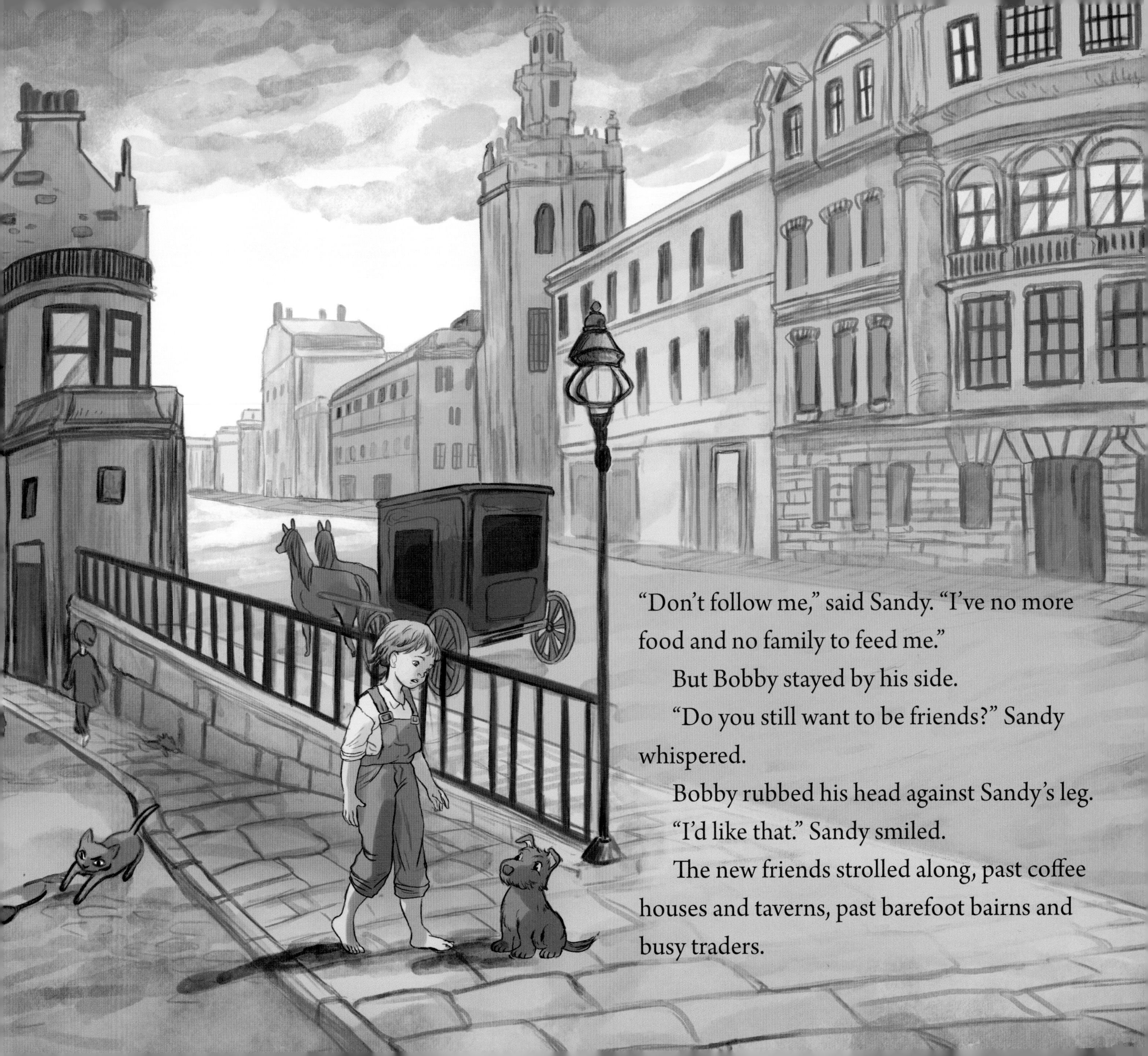

"Don't follow me," said Sandy. "I've no more food and no family to feed me."

But Bobby stayed by his side.

"Do you still want to be friends?" Sandy whispered.

Bobby rubbed his head against Sandy's leg.

"I'd like that." Sandy smiled.

The new friends strolled along, past coffee houses and taverns, past barefoot bairns and busy traders.

Sandy stopped at the bakery window.

"What fine cakes," he said. "I'd love a ginger bun, wouldn't you? If only I had a penny."

But Bobby wasn't looking at the cakes. He was looking across the street… at a boy with his hand in a gentleman's pocket… a boy who was stealing a watch! Bobby started barking loud and shrill.

Quick as a flash, the pickpocket shot off, with Bobby bounding after him and Sandy chasing along behind.

Helter-skelter up the winding street
they ran after the pickpocket,
wriggling past skirts and boots...

dodging wheels and hooves,
bounding uphill at full pelt.

The thief was just a whisker from Bobby's bite when…

90

... stramash!

They ran straight into the path of Constable John Gray, who was working late that morning.

"Bobby!" said John in surprise. "What's all this?"

"That laddie stole a pocket watch!" shouted Sandy, breathless. "This wee dog saw him do it!"

Bobby barked and tugged at the pickpocket's sleeve, and a glittering gold chain and watch slithered out onto the ground.

"Well done Bobby!" said Constable John Gray.

"That's my pocket watch," said a gentleman, stepping forward. It was the headmaster from Heriot's school. "It's our favourite rat-catcher!" He ruffled the puppy's fur. "Thank you wee Bobby. You can visit our kitchen for a sausage any time you like!" Bobby wagged his tail.

"And you, laddie." He turned to Sandy. "What would you like as a reward?"

Sandy stood on his tiptoes and whispered in the man's ear. "To play marbles and hoops with the other boys."

The headmaster peered at Sandy with his ragged clothes and his bare feet.

And then, he smiled.

One frosty morning the next week, a meaty waft of sizzling sausages drifted down to the Grassmarket.

Bobby flew up the steps, past Constable John Gray, squeezed through the railings of Heriot's school and bolted across the yard.

Weaving his way through the playground games he heard a familiar voice.

"Hello wee Bobby!" shouted Sandy, running over to give his friend a pat.

Bobby wagged his tail and leaped.

"Sandy, come back and play!" the other boys called.

"I've got to go now, Bobby," said Sandy, smiling, "but I'll see you soon."

When evening came, Bobby plodded wearily back down the steps to his grubby straw bed. His tummy was full, but he was all alone. He longed for a home and a family of his own as he shivered beneath the cold moon.

The next day, Bobby pulled himself up, had a shake and a stretch, and trotted up the steps.

He didn't squeeze through the railings. He didn't visit the school. He carried on up to the top, where he sat and waited.

Wee Bobby had a plan.

Trudging towards him came Constable John Gray, who was on his way home from work.

"Good morning wee Bobby," he said. "Waiting for me, are you? No sausages at the school today?"

Bobby wagged his tail and woofed.

"Ever thought of being a watchdog, Bobby?" asked John Gray. "You'd be braw company on my lonely night shift."

Bobby wagged his tail and whirled.

"What do you say, will you join me?"

And when John Gray turned to go, Bobby followed.

On dark Edinburgh nights from then on, a wee Skye terrier patrolled the cobbled streets with his master, the night watchman. Together they looked out for fires, caught thieves and kept the sleeping city safe.

90

And when morning came, side by side, they headed for home, a soft, warm bed – and sometimes sausages for breakfast.

It is said that when John Gray became a night watchman, he took on Bobby, a wee Skye terrier pup, as his watchdog.

After John Gray died in 1858, the loyal little dog lay beside his master's grave in Greyfriars kirkyard every day for fourteen years. He became known as Greyfriars Bobby.

Each day when Bobby heard the One O'clock Gun firing from Edinburgh Castle, he would leave the kirkyard to visit his master's favourite coffee house, where the staff gave him lunch.

Bobby became so well loved in Edinburgh that the Lord Provost himself paid for Bobby's dog licence and presented him with a special collar.

When Bobby died in 1872, aged sixteen, he too was buried in Greyfriars kirkyard, not far from his beloved master's grave.

Today visitors come from all over the
world to see Bobby's statue in Edinburgh,
and to lay flowers and sticks on his grave.

GLOSSARY

bairns: children
braw: good
dreich: dreary, miserable
helter-skelter: moving quickly and wildly
kirkyard: churchyard
laddie: boy
stramash: smash, crash
wee: small

To Al and Kay, with love – M.S.

To my little friend Charlie the dog,
who helped me when I was a child – E.B.

Kelpies is an imprint of Floris Books
First published in 2019 by Floris Books

The publisher acknowledges subsidy from Creative Scotland towards the publication of this volume

British Library CIP data available. ISBN 978-178250-590-7
Printed in Malta by Gutenberg Press Ltd